Mysterious Spots

by Linda Diaz
illustrated by Nancy White Cassidy

Harcourt
SCHOOL PUBLISHERS

Printed in China

ISBN 10: 0-15-350521-4
ISBN 13: 978-0-15-350521-8

Ordering Options
ISBN 10: 0-15-350334-3 (Grade 4 Below-Level Collection)
ISBN 13: 978-0-15-350334-4 (Grade 4 Below-Level Collection)
ISBN 10: 0-15-357511-5 (package of 5)
ISBN 13: 978-0-15-357511-2 (package of 5)

11 12 13 14 15   0940   12 11 10

"Finky, sit," commanded Tanya. School was over for the day. Tanya was giving her dog, Finky, a treat but making certain the dog earned it first. Finky sat on the kitchen floor and looked up at Tanya.

"That's a good boy," Tanya said and tossed him a dog biscuit.

The family had adopted Finky in September. Now it was January. Tanya put a leash on Finky, and she put on her own coat, hat, and mittens. She told her mom she was going to take Finky for a walk.

Tanya's family lived in a large city. So, Finky didn't get to run through large fields like some dogs. Tanya tried to make up for this by giving him two or three walks each day. Today, there was a hint of snow in the air.

Finky walked down the sidewalk, sniffing everything he could reach. When any other dogs or people approached, he became very timid. Finky would usually hide behind Tanya. He was a mutt, a mix of several kinds of dogs, with drab, gray-brown fur and white spots.

After their walk, Tanya turned to Finky and started to pet him. Something looked a little different about Finky, though. His white spots seemed to be bigger.

"Mom, Finky's spots look bigger!" called Tanya.

"That's because he's still young, and his body's still growing and changing," said her mother.

"I'm talking about just today, though. His spots look bigger than they did after school," said Tanya. She turned Finky over to examine his other side. Those spots looked bigger than before, too. She didn't think much more about it and went to do her homework.

Tanya woke up early the next morning. She was thrilled to see that it was snowing. On their walk, Finky seemed excited, too. He ran up and down the sidewalk and licked at some of the snowflakes.

"Come on, Finky, time to go in," Tanya called after a while. She didn't want Finky's feet to get too cold. When they got back to the apartment, Tanya dried off Finky's fur. She noticed that his white spots seemed even larger than they had the night before.

"This is very peculiar," Tanya said.

The snow continued all day long. Tanya went outside to enjoy it with her friend, Jenny. She was surprised by how much it was snowing. Sometimes, her city would get a good snowfall. But this was the biggest one Tanya had ever seen.

By five o'clock in the afternoon, there were at least nine inches of snow on the ground. Tanya looked out on to the street below. She saw people shoveling their sidewalks and brushing snow off of their cars.

Tanya's father didn't get home that evening until late. The heavy snow made traveling slow and difficult. "I've been sitting in the car forever," he said, taking off his boots.

Finky dashed up to him, wagging his tail. As her father petted him, Tanya looked at Finky. She thought once again that Finky's white spots were definitely larger than they used to be. No one else seemed to notice and everyone was distracted by the storm. So she decided not to say anything about it.

Tanya's mother and father turned on the television to see the news about the snow. "More snow is coming?" her father asked, frustrated.

The next morning, it was still snowing—and snowing hard! Tanya looked across at the roof next door. She was fascinated by the tall pile of snow on it. Tanya picked up Finky and held him so that he could look out the window.

"Look, there's even more snow for us to play in, boy!" she said. Then she noticed that Finky's white spots were even bigger!

Jenny called Tanya, and they took Finky outside together. They walked down the block looking at all the beautiful snow. Many neighbors were out shoveling. Everyone was talking about the enormous snowstorm. Finky hopped through the deeper snow that wasn't shoveled yet. The girls walked along, throwing snowballs and gazing at the lovely snow.

"Fifteen inches so far, and more to come!" said Angelo, their neighbor down the block. Tanya and Jenny looked at each other with amazement.

"They're saying it could snow like this for another day or so," said Tanya's mother. She was sitting in front of the television when Tanya and Finky came home. The weather reporter on TV was saying that the snowfall could set a record if the storm continued.

"We need to go to the store for groceries," said her mother. The trip to the store and back took a very long time. Many people were stocking up on groceries to ride out the storm.

When they got home, Finky came running up to them. Tanya was shocked to see that Finky was now almost completely white! Tanya trembled with fear. "How could this be happening?" she thought to herself.

"Let's put these groceries away," said her mother. They filled up the cabinets and refrigerator with food and supplies. They would be living like hermits until the storm passed. Afterward, her mother turned on the TV to check on the storm. Tanya didn't want to bother her about Finky. Her mother had more important concerns on her mind. Besides, she was still the only one who seemed to notice the change in Finky.

Tanya's mother and father were especially worried about the storm. They wanted to be able to get to work in the morning. Tanya was nervous about Finky. She wondered if he would be all right. When the snow first fell, Tanya was happy and excited. But now things seemed strange. She went to bed that night with Finky at her side, feeling troubled.

The next morning, Tanya woke up to a room filled with sunshine. Sunshine meant that the snow had stopped! Sure enough, there was blue sky and not a flake of snow falling. "Hurrah, Finky, the big storm is over!" Tanya said.

Tanya couldn't believe what she saw. Finky wasn't white anymore. His drab gray-brown fur and white spots were back to normal. She hugged Finky and said, "Everything will be okay now, Finky!" Then she thought to herself, "Just as long as it does not snow again!"

Think Critically

1. How do Finky's spots and the snowstorm seem to be tied together? What seemed to cause the snowstorm?

2. How would you describe Finky?

3. What word means almost the same thing as *trembled* does on page 12?

4. How did Tanya feel about Finky's spots growing larger?

5. What did you find surprising in this story? Why?

 Language Arts

Write a Poem Make a list of words that describe a snowy day like the one in the story. Look at the pictures in the story for some ideas. Then write a poem about a snowy day, using some of the words from your list.

School-Home Connection Share this story with family members or friends. Then ask if they have ever experienced a big snowstorm. If so, have them talk about what they did during the storm.

Word Count: 1,042